The Song Within My Heart

Nokum Relaxing, 51 cm x 41 cm (20" x 16"), 2000

Allen Sapp

The Song Within My Heart

DAVID BOUCHARD
the art of ALLEN SAPP
the music of NORTHERN CREE

Red Deer Press

Listen to the beating drum
It tells a hundred stories
Of our people, of our homeland
Some of birds and beasts and sweet grass.

Close your eyes and listen
You might come to hear a story
That no one hears but you alone
A story of your very own.

Nitohtaw ana mistikiwaskihk ka-pakamahot
e-witak ana mitahtatomitanaw acimowinisa
Kitayisiniminowak ekwa kitaskinaw ohci
Atiht peyisisak, pisiskowak ekwa wihkaskwa

Kipaha kiskisikwa ekwa nitohta
Apwetikwe acimowinis kapeten
Kiya piko epeyakowiyan ewis-petaman
Kiya kitacimowin

The Man Singing While She's Doing Beads, 61 cm x 46 cm (24" x 18"), 1990

An Indoor Pow-Wow, 46 cm x 61 cm (18" x 24"), 1995

Allen Sapp

Listen to the singers
They are also telling stories
Some of pleasure, some of sorrow
Some of birth or life here after.

Close your eyes and listen
You might come to hear a story
That no one hears but you alone
Another of your very own.

Nitohtaw aniki nikamowinowak
Wistawa e-acimocik
Atiht ohci e-miyowatakik, atiht e-pikwetakik
Atiht nihtawikiwin ekwa pimatisiwin

Kipa kisikiskwa ekwa nitohta
Apwetikwe acimowinis kapeten
Kiya piko epeyakowiyan ewis-petaman
Kotak mina kiya kitacimowin

HI hey hey hey HEY hey hi
hey HI hey hey he
I hey hey hey HI hey hey hey HEY hey hey!

When at first I heard them
I was standing near my Nokum
I stood staring at my elder
Who was lost somewhere in deepest thought.

Aspiwiye e-petaman
Ciki eki-nipawistawak awa nohkom
E-kikanawapamak awa okiskikemo
Mitoni ewanisik omamtoneyicikan

Allen Sapp

When at first I heard them
I was standing with my Nokum
Who smiled and began swaying
Closed her eyes and started singing.
Not loud at first, a simple hum
I tugged with force on both her arms.

Aspiwiye e-petaman
Ciki eki-nipawistawak awa nohkom
E-pahpapisit ekwa e-maci nanimihtopayisit
Kipaham oskisikwa ekwa e-maci nikamot
Namoya mitonisi ekisiwet-tepiyak apsis e-nikomosit
Ewaskocipitak nanpo ospitona

Allen Sapp

Allen Sopp

hey.he

"Grandma," I called out to her
"I don't know what they're saying!"
She couldn't or she didn't hear
Yet I was loud and she was near?

"Grandma," I yelled out again
"Please tell me what they're saying."
She smiled as she looked down at me
And taught me how to hear and see.

"Nohkom" esi tehpwatak
"Namoya anima ekiskeyitaman tansi eyitwecik"
Namoy nipetak
Ata ekisiweyan ekwa cikik e-ayat.

"Nohkom" kitwam e-tepweyan
"mahtesa witamowin tansi eyitwecik"
Ki-pahpisiw ekwa ekanawapamit
E-kiskinohamowit tansi Ka-petaman ekwa kawapatamon

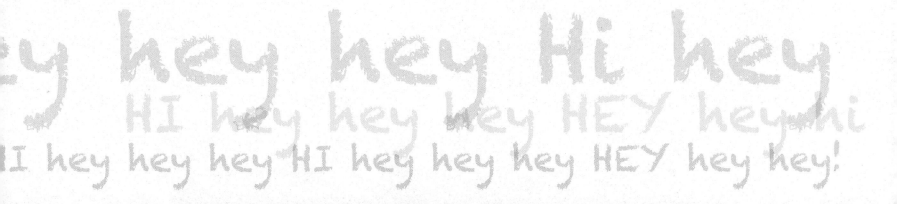

Allen Sapp

"Child," she said, "There are some things
That you can call your very own.
Not toys or clothes, not jewels or cars
Don't ever make these things your own."

"Nosim" ayitwet
Mintoni kakitwan kiya ohi
Namoya mecawakanisa, ayiwinisa, wawesewakana, jehkiwak
Kiya wikac ekosi kitwan akoni kiya

"There aren't a lot but there are things
That you should learn to call your own.
Your stories, songs and beating heart
Are truly yours and yours alone."

"Namoya mistahi kikway maka atiht
Kakitwan ekoni anihi kiya
Kitacimowinsa, nikamowina, ekwa kinanamiteh
Kiyanihi ekoni, kiya piko"

Allen Sapp

And right there at that pow-wow
(Nokum knew the time for teaching)
The scorching sun echoed the drums
The dancers would be soon to come.

"Yes child," she said. "There are some things
That you can call your very own.
Your stories, songs and beating heart
Are truly yours and yours alone."

Ekwa ekota anima pwatisimowin
(Nohkom kiskeyitam tanispi kaki-kiskinohamaket)
Kisastew awa pisim mitoni e-cistakepitat
  anihi mistikwaskikwa
Wipac onimihitowak wipeyitsimowak

"Eha nosim" eyisit awa nohkom, "Atiht kikway
Kakitwan ekoni anihi kiya
Kitacimowinsa, nikamowina, ekwa kinanamiteh
Kiyanihi ekoni, kiya piko"

At The Pow-Wow, 30 cm x 41 cm (12" x 16"), 1985

HÍ

ey hey!

Summer Pow-Wow, 61 cm x 91 cm (24" x 36"), 2002

Allen Sapp

HEY hey hey
Hi hey hey hey
HI hey hey hey
HEY hey hi.

HEY hey hey
Hi hey hey hey
HI hey hey hey
HEY hey hey!

"A story is a sacred thing
That should be passed from age to youth
I choose to share my best with you
That you might own and share them too."

"And never use another's tale
Unless he knows and he approves.
And only then and then alone
Might you tell it to others."

"Acimowin peyakwan kakisimowin
Kakikwe kaspotak ohi oskayak ohci
Ekwa enawasonaman ohi tatwa anihi kamiyowasiki
Apwetikwe awiyak kaki apacitaw"

"Ekwa kaya wikac apacita kotak awiyak otacimowinis
Kispin piko ekiskeyitakik ekwa etapowakeyitakik
Ekota piko kaki asonamowaw
Kotak awiyak"

Allen Sopp

The Man Is Going To Sing A Song, 41 cm x 30 cm (16" x 12"), 1992

Allen Sapp

BOOM bo
BOOM
BOOM

"And much the same, the beating drum
It echoes that which is your soul
You seek a rhythm that is true
Of all the secrets that are you."

"So much of what the drummer feels
Is clear with every beat you hear.
He bears it all, he cannot hide.
He's sharing what he is inside."

"Ekwa peyakewan ana mistikwaskihk
Esakwet ekota ahcahk
Kamisken nikamon etapwetaman
Ekwa ekecinamowin anima kiya"

"Mistikwaskihk ana kapakamahot
Mosita ana nikamowino
Kiwapatihik, namoya kaki-kataw
E-witamask tanisi etamacihot"

Allen Sapp

"And of the things in my own life
That I have owned, there are none so dear
As songs I sing and stories tell
All tales that you should know by now."

"To understand the song I sing
Close your eyes and listen
And try to hear the subtle things
It is your Nokum's heart that sings."

"Kakiyaw anihi kakitipeyitaman ni-pimatisiwin
Piko kikway kakitopeyitaman, namkikway nisahkiten ayiwak
Ispici nikamona ekwa acimowina
Kaki-kiskeyitaman asay"

"Ka-nistohtaman anihi nikamowinsa ka-nikamoyan
Kipaha kiskisikwa ekwa nitohta
Kakwe-nitohta
Apo ci ana kohkom oteha e-nikamot"

If you, dear reader, hear me sing
And can't make out my message.
You should not fret, I was like you
I had to learn to listen too!

To understand the song I sing
Close your eyes and listen
And try to hear the subtle things
It's of my Nokum that I sing.

"Kispin kiya otayamicikewihina kipetawin enikamoyan
Ekwa namoya e-nistohtowiyin
Kiya ka-wanoteyiten, peyakwan nista
Eki-nistohtamowikowiyan tansi kisipetaman nista"

Ka-nitohtaman anihi nikamowinsa ka-nikmoyan
Kipaha kiskisikwan ekwa nitohta
Kakwe-nitohta
Nohkom ana ohci ka-nikamoyan

I hey

Nokum's Tender Love, 61 cm x 46 cm (24" x 18"), 2002

Allen Sapp

My Nokum, Maggie Soonias

Me (second from left) with my father Alex and my sister and three brothers

Allen Sapp

A note from
the painter...

I like to go to pow-wows and experience the renewal of soul and body which happens there. Pow-wows are a time of happiness with the songs telling a story and the dancers adding to the excitement. Dancing with other people from near and far brings me closer to my people. This is a time for young and old to get together in friendship and happiness.

Our old people have much to teach us if we will only listen. In my own life I remember with deep gratitude the influence my Nokum — my grandmother — had on me. I liked to draw while I was in school and sometimes the teacher would hand out one of my drawings as a prize for the rest of the children. One time I asked Nokum if I could draw her and she said, "Sure, go ahead and do it." She told me that if I kept at my drawing I would be very happy some day. And I remember her words of advice: "Don't do stupid things, like getting involved with alcohol and drugs."

I have often painted my Nokum making bannock, feeding the chickens or doing bead work. I would help her feed the chickens and go into the hen house to gather up eggs. I only went to school for a short time and although I never learned to read and write my Nokum and my father Alex taught me to show respect, not only for the people but for everything that Manito has put on the earth. That is why when we go to pow-wows to dance we also offer thanks to the good earth, the animals, the birds and nature, which provide for all of our needs. I am happy that for thirty years I have been able to paint scenes from my childhood on the reserve and share the beauty that Manito has created with all people.

Parents and grandparents must teach young people the important things in life and help to preserve our culture so that Indian people will be proud of their heritage. My father said I should thank Manito as I wake in the morning and before I go to sleep at night. He used to sing to me and one of my fondest memories is when he took me to my first pow-wow and while resting on his shoulders I heard the beat of the drums. He also encouraged me to let my hair grow long, to show people that I was a Naheyow, an Indian.

To Maggie Soonias, who encouraged me to paint and inspired me to do my best.   ALLEN SAPP

I would like to acknowledge the presence and contribution of my friend James Kurtz,
the late son of John and Monica Kurtz. James was so present in so much of this.   DAVID BOUCHARD

Text copyright © 2015 David Bouchard
Illustrations copyright © 2015 Allen Sapp
Music copyright © 2015 Northern Cree

Published in Canada by Red Deer Press,
195 Allstate Parkway, Markham, Ontario L3R 4T8

Published in the United States by Red Deer Press,
311 Washington Street, Brighton, Massachusetts 02135

All inquiries should be addressed to Red Deer Press,
195 Allstate Parkway, Markham, Ontario L3R 4T8.
reddeerpress.com

10 9 8 7 6 5 4 3 2 1

Red Deer Press acknowledges with thanks the Canada Council for the Arts, and the Ontario Arts Council
for their support of our publishing program. We acknowledge the financial support of the
Government of Canada through the Canada Book Fund (CBF) for our publishing activities.

Library and Archives Canada Cataloguing in Publication
Bouchard, David
Song within my heart / David Bouchard ; illustrated by Allen Sapp
ISBN 978-0-88995-500-4
Data available on file.

Publisher Cataloguing-in-Publication Data (U.S.)
Bouchard, David
Song within my heart / David Bouchard ; illustrated by Allen Sapp
ISBN 978-0-88995-500-4
Data available on file.

Originally published in 2002 in a different format as ISBN 9781551925592

Cree Translation: Steve Wood
Cover and interior design by Tanya Montini
Printed in China by Sheck Wah Tong Printing Press Ltd.